THE FAMOUS FIVE

SHORT STORIES

GOOD OLD TIMMY

The Famous Five

Timmy   Anne   Dick   Julian   George

Text copyright © Enid Blyton, 1956
Illustrations copyright © Jamie Littler, 2014

Enid Blyton's signature is a registered trade mark of Hodder & Stoughton Ltd

Text first published in Great Britain in Enid Blyton's Magazine Annual – No. 3, in 1956.
Also available in The Famous Five Short Stories, published by Hodder Children's Books.
First published in Great Britain in this edition in 2014 by Hodder Children's Books

1

A Catalogue record for this book is available from the British Library
ISBN 978 1 444 91630 0

Hodder Children's Books
A division of Hachette Children's Books
Hachette UK Limited, 338 Euston Road, London NW1 3BH

www.hachette.co.uk

Enid Blyton
GOOD OLD TIMMY

illustrated by **Jamie Littler**

Hodder Children's Books

A division of Hachette Children's Books

Famous Five Colour Reads

For a complete list of the full-length
Famous Five adventures, turn to
the last page of this book

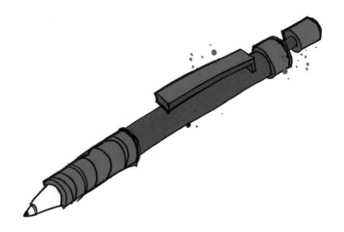

Contents

CHAPTER ONE

'Aren't you ready to come down to the
beach and swim, Anne?' yelled George,
standing at the bottom of the stairs.
'We're all waiting for you.
HURRY UP!'

The study door flew open
and Mr Kirrin, George's father, appeared.
**'Georgina! Will you stop
shouting all day long?** How can I
work? For pity's sake, clear out of the house.'

'We're just going, Dad – and we're taking a picnic lunch so we won't be disturbing you for some time. I know you're on a big job – it's bad luck it's holiday time and we're here!'

He grunted and disappeared into his study. George's mother appeared with two big bags of sandwiches.

'Oh dear – was that your father shouting again?' she said. 'Never mind! He **doesn't mean to be bad-tempered** – but he really is on a big job at the moment, and he's trying to get some figures for **the scientist** he's working with, a **Professor Humes,** who's staying in **Kirrin** – at the **Rollins Hotel.** Now – here are your sandwiches – and biscuits and apples – and you can take some bottles of ginger beer out of the larder.'

Just then Anne raced down the stairs, and **the Five,** all in their swimming things, went off to the beach to swim and laze and play games on the sands.

Only three people were there – **two men** and a lonely looking **boy.** Julian found a shaded cave and put the food on a shelf of rock.

'What about a swim straight away?' he said. 'Look – Timmy's off to rub noses with that **dog** we saw yesterday – the big ugly one we didn't much like. **He belongs to those two men.** They're not much to look at either! I wouldn't like to meet them on a dark night!'

'Well, Timmy seems to **like** their dog all right,' said George, staring at the two dogs **sniffing** at one another, then tearing along the sands together, **barking happily.**

CHAPTER TWO.

'Look,' said Dick, 'there's that kid coming along the beach again. Shall we ask him to come swimming with us – he seems to be all on his own. **Look out, kid – don't get knocked over by our dog!'**

Timmy had come racing up joyfully, **chasing the other dog,** and the **boy** went **sprawling** as they galloped round him. Timmy turned in surprise and saw the boy *rolling over and over* on the sand. He gave an apologetic bark, and ran to the small boy, licking and sniffing at him.

The boy was **terrified of Timmy.** He began to **scream** in terror, and Julian ran to him.

'He's only making friends, he's only saying **he's SORRY** he **knocked you over, he WON'T hurt you!** Come on, get up – we were just going to ask you to come and swim with us.'

'Oh,' said the boy, and
stood up, shaking the sand off
himself. He looked to be about nine or ten,
and small for his age. 'Well – thanks. I'd like
to swim with you. I'm **Oliver Humes,**
and I'm staying at the **Rollins Hotel.'**

'Then your dad must be a friend of our uncle,' said Dick. 'He's called Kirrin – **Quentin Kirrin** – and he's a scientist. So is your dad, isn't he?'

'Yes. A very good one too,' said Oliver proudly. 'But he's **worried this morning.'**

'Why? What's up?' said George.

'Well – he's working on something important,' said Oliver, 'and this morning he had a **horrible letter.** It said that unless Dad agreed to **give the writer information** he wanted about what Dad was working on,

he'd –
he'd kidnap me!'

CHAPTER THREE

'**Oh rubbish!**' said Julian. '**Don't you worry** about that! We'll tell our dog Timmy to look after you. Just look at him playing with that ugly great mongrel. Timmy's a mongrel too – but we think he's beautiful!'

'I think he's too big,' said Oliver,
fearfully, as Timmy came running up, panting.

The other dog went back to the
two men, who had just whistled for him.

'Come on –
let's swim,' said Dick.
'I **can't** swim,' said
Oliver. 'I wish you'd teach me.'

'Right. We will when
we've had our swim,' said Anne.
'We'll go into the water now.
Come on!'

29

And soon **the Five,** Timmy too, were splashing in the sea, yelling and diving in and out, having a glorious time, while Oliver **paddled near the shore.**

Then suddenly
Julian gave a **shout,**
and **pointed** to **the beach.**
'**Look!** What's happening there?
Hey!'

31

All **the Five** looked, and saw something very surprising! **The two men** who owned the big brown dog were **dragging Oliver** out of the water, one with his hand over the boy's mouth.

'They're **kidnapping him!** Remember that **threatening letter** he told us about, that his dad got this morning? Come on, **quick** – see if we can **stop them. TIMMY!** Come on, **now!**'

CHAPTER FOUR

They **swam to the shore** and slipped hurriedly into their sandals.

'They've taken the **kid up the cliffs** – they're at **the top, look!'** panted Julian. **'After them, Timmy!'**

But not even Timmy
could get up the cliffs in time to
rescue the **screaming boy. Julian**
was at the top first, with Timmy – just
in time to see **a car driving off.**

The **big dog** was **galloping after it.**

'Why didn't they take the dog in the car,
too?' wondered Dick.

'Perhaps he's a **car-sick dog?**' said Anne. 'Anyway, I bet he knows where the men are going, and has been **ordered to follow.** If the car doesn't go too fast he can easily keep up.'

'I've got **the number,** anyway,' said Dick. 'Listen – I think **Anne's right** when she says the dog must know where the men are going,' said Julian. 'And it **can't** be **far away** if the dog has to **run the whole distance.'**

Timmy wasn't listening. He was sniffing the ground here and there. Then he suddenly began to **trot along the cliff-road, nose** to ground.

George gave a sudden exclamation.

'I know! He's **sniffing** the other **dog's tracks** – he knows his smell, and he's **following it!'**

'You're right! Look – let's see if he'll follow the trail properly,' said Julian. 'He might lead us **to Oliver!** Tell him, George. He always understands every word you say.'

'Timmy! Listen!' said George, and pointed to some paw marks made in the sandy road by the big mongrel dog. **'Follow, Timmy, follow.** Understand?'

Timmy lifted his big head and looked hard at George, his ears pricked up, his head on one side. *Yes – he understood.*

Then, with nose to ground, he trotted swiftly away down the cliff-road, sniffing the tracks of the other dog. How did he do it?

What a nose Timmy had!

'Come on,' said Dick. 'Timmy will lead us to wherever those men are taking Oliver.'

CHAPTER FIVE

Very steadily, **Timmy followed the scent** down the cliff-road, turned off to the left, trotted down a lane, swung to the right, then to the left.

He **waited** at the traffic lights,

and when they changed to green, **he crossed** the road,

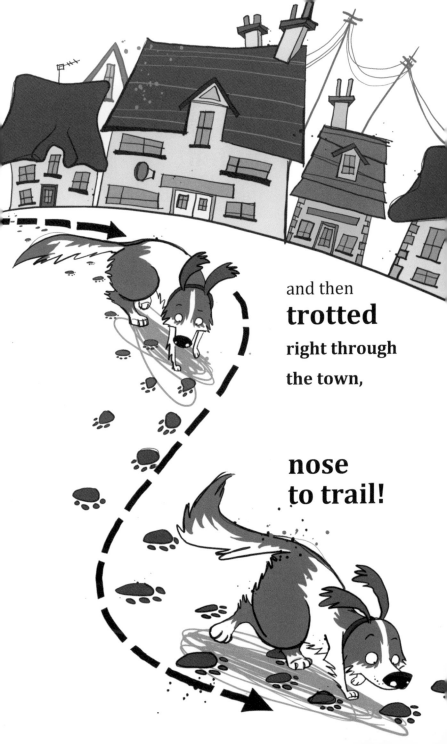

and then **trotted** right through the town,

nose to trail!

The children padded behind in their swimming things, Anne getting **very puffed!**

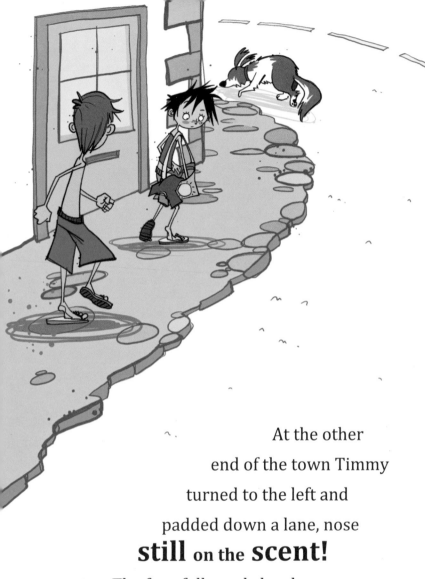

At the other
end of the town Timmy
turned to the left and
padded down a lane, nose
still on the scent!
The four followed closely.

'I'll have to have a rest soon,'
panted Anne.

'Hey, that's **the car** that **took** the **boy away!**' exclaimed Dick, suddenly, as they passed a garage, outside which stood a black car, taking in petrol. 'The men are in it. But **I can't see Oliver** – and that great dog isn't anywhere about, either.'

'Well, they must have **hidden Oliver** somewhere not far off, and then they came back here for petrol,' said Julian. 'Go on, Tim – you're on the right trail. I expect they've left that **dog** in charge of the **boy.** I bet if anyone went near, he'd **tear them to pieces!**'

'And I **don't** want Timmy in a **dogfight,'** said George.

'Yes. Not so good,' said Julian, and came to a stop. Timmy, however, went on, and **wouldn't come back,** even though George called him.

'Obstinate thing!' said George crossly. 'Once he's **following a trail nothing** on earth will **stop him.** Well – I'm going after him in case he gets into trouble!'

'Look – Timmy's gone through that gateway,' said Anne, 'into a field. There's **a shed** at the bottom of it. Could Oliver be there, with the dog inside, guarding him?'

Timmy **stopped** suddenly and began **to growl.** George ran to catch hold of his collar. But Timmy wrenched himself away and **raced** **to the shed,** scraping at the wooden door. Immediately a volley of **fierce** **barks** came from the shed. **The Five** halted. A voice came from the shed.

'Help! Help,
       I'm locked in here!'

CHAPTER SIX

'There – Timmy **followed** the trail **correctly!**' said George. 'Quick, Ju – we mustn't let him break in that door – the other dog will fly at him, and at us, too! **Whatever can we do?'**

It was obvious that the other dog had been left **on guard,** and would **fling** himself on anyone or anything that tried to prevent him from doing his duty.

'TIMMY! STOP THROWING YOURSELF AGAINST THAT DOOR!' yelled George. **'YOU'LL BREAK IT DOWN, AND THEN GOODNESS KNOWS WHAT'LL HAPPEN!'**

As both dogs, barking **fiercely,** again **flung** themselves on it from **opposite sides**, the **door cracked** in **two** places – and the bottom half shook **and** shivered!

'Anne, George, **quick, come with me!**' said Julian. 'We may **be attacked by that dog** once he **gets out! Run!** We could perhaps climb that tree, look! **Hurry up, for goodness' sake!**'

Terrified,
they all raced
for the tree,
and clambered
up on the
branches.

CRASH!

The door **fell to the ground, broken in half.** At once **the great** mongrel **leapt out.**

But it took absolutely **no notice of Timmy.** It ran instead to the tree and stood below, **growling fiercely.**

Timmy stood staring in surprise. Why was this dog growling at the children? It was all **a mistake,** Timmy decided, and he must put it right.

He ran to the tree, and whined as if to say: *'It's all right. Please **come down** and **play with us!'** * Then he went to the other dog, and whined to him too.

The mongrel gave a loud bark, and jumped up. He ran off a little, stopped and turned round as if saying to Timmy: *'All right – you want a game? Then so do I! You're the dog I **played** with this morning, aren't you? Well, come on, **let's have a game!'**

And, to the children's enormous astonishment the two dogs gambolled amiably together!

CHAPTER SEVEN

'I feel a bit silly up here,' said Dick, climbing down. 'Come on – the war's over. Those dogs look as if they're friends for life. Let's go and **get that kid.**'

With the **frightened boy** safely in their midst, they began **to walk** **cautiously** out of the field.

The two dogs took absolutely **no notice!** The big mongrel had got Timmy down on the ground, and was pretending to worry him. Timmy was having the **time of his life!**

'Look – there's a **bus** going to **Kirrin!**' said Julian, delighted. **'Stop it!** We'll get in and take Oliver **back to safety** while we've a chance. Timmy will just have to walk. He'll make that dog **forget** all about **guarding Oliver!'**

It wasn't very long before they
were safely back in Kirrin. Oliver looked
very white, but when Julian told him
solemnly that it was really **a very big
adventure,** he cheered up and began
to boast!

'I was **kidnapped!** What will the boys at school say? But I was really scared though. Can we go and find my dad?'

Professor Humes was **very** thankful to see his son again, for already he had notified **the police** that he **had disappeared.** Dick gave the police **the number** of the men's car.

'You'll soon track that all right!' he said. 'But not as well as Tim here – he used his nose, and **a very good nose it is too!'**

'Woof!' said Timmy, and let his tongue hang out of his mouth.

'He says he's hot and thirsty,' said George. 'Let's buy him an ice-cream.'

'We'll **ALL** have the **biggest ice-creams** there are in the village shop,' said the Professor, patting Timmy. 'I could do with one myself.'

'I could do with four,' said Oliver, 'so I hope you're feeling generous, Dad! Dad, Timmy's a **wonder dog!'**

'Well, we've always known that,' said George. **'Come on, Timmy – ICE-CREAMS!'**

If you enjoyed this Famous Five short story, there's plenty more action and adventure in the full-length Famous Five novels. Here is a list of all the titles, in the order they were first published.

1. Five On A Treasure Island
2. Five Go Adventuring Again
3. Five Run Away Together
4. Five Go to Smuggler's Top
5. Five Go Off in a Caravan
6. Five On Kirrin Island Again
7. Five Go Off to Camp
8. Five Get Into Trouble
9. Five Fall Into Adventure
10. Five on a Hike Together
11. Five Have a Wonderful Time
12. Five Go Down to the Sea
13. Five Go to Mystery Moor
14. Five Have Plenty of Fun
15. Five on a Secret Trail
16. Five Go to Billycock Hill
17. Five Get Into a Fix
18. Five on Finniston Farm
19. Five Go to Demon's Rocks
20. Five Have a Mystery to Solve
21. Five Are Together Again